# Kristına Takes the Stage

Written by Lisa Bullard

Illustrations by John Carrozza

THE FRIENDS FOREVER GIRLS™ COLLECTION

Created by **Kristi L. Necochea**

Thank you for choosing to read
*Kristina Takes the Stage.*
It's been my dream to create
The Friends Forever Girls™ collection
of dolls and books, and I hope you
like them as much as I do!

Kristi L. Necochea

Questions or comments? Visit our Website at
FriendsForeverGirls.com

ISBN-13: 978-0-9792361-2-9 softcover

Library of Congress Control Number: 2008921840

Manufactured in the United States of America
1  2  3  4  5  6  –  BP  –  13  12  11  10  09  08

*For Randi, and for Phyllis ~ L.B.*

# Chapter One

**Thunk! One minute** Kristina was leaning forward on the bench. Next thing she knew, it had tipped over. She landed on the stage with a thump. She had been concentrating hard, trying to remember her next line of dialogue. Now all the other actors were staring at her.

"Uh– I forgot my line," she said.

Kristina felt her cheeks burning. If only these things didn't always happen to her! But then she noticed her new friend Marlee winking at her. Another friend, Kyleen, smiled and held out a hand. Kristina grabbed it and stood up.

"Good thing I didn't break my funny bone," she said loudly, "since my part in the play is supposed to get lots of laughs."

The other students grinned. Drama Club was one of Kristina's favorite things about her new school. Not long before, her family had moved across town to a bigger house. At first, all Kristina could think about was how much she missed her friends at her old school. Now she had all sorts of new friends because of Drama Club.

And she had the play to look forward to. Kristina loved practices. The singing and dancing made her feel like a superstar. She could hardly wait to perform in front of a real audience. The auditorium seats would be filled with moms and dads, brothers and sisters, students and teachers. And they'd all laugh when Kristina said the funny things her character was supposed to say.

That is, if she could remember her lines! Somehow, as hard as she tried, they kept slipping out of her head. It was kind of like taking a test. Even when she studied hard, she still forgot the answers. But when it came to the play, she was lucky. The other kids did not make fun of her mistakes. And Marlee and Kyleen practiced with Kristina whenever she asked. Marlee never missed her lines. And Kyleen was the best singer and dancer in Drama Club. But they were always willing to help Kristina.

Marlee and Kyleen had also shared with her

the Butterfly Promises:

> **B**e the best I can be
> **U**se kindness and be fair
> **T**ell the truth
> **T**reat others the way I want to be treated
> **E**ncourage my friends
> **R**espect myself and others
> **F**ind the courage to do what's right
> **L**isten to others
>    and remember...
> **Y**ou can do it!

Believing that their friendships would last forever, Marlee and Kyleen together with the other Friends Forever Girls, Nika, Reina and Natalie pledged to use the Butterfly Promises to guide their actions and friendships with each other. It was starting to seem like her family's move was the best thing that had ever happened to her.

"Alright actors," said the play's director, Ms. Tyler, "we'll stop for today. Remember to turn in your hats so they're all here tomorrow." She added, "Kristina, may I see you a moment?"

Kristina felt her stomach sinking as she turned away from Kyleen. Was Ms. Tyler going to lecture her about forgetting her lines?

"Yes, Ms. Tyler?"

"Kristina, I hope you understand that the backstage jobs are just as important as the acting. We agreed that your special job is to take care of the hats. But yesterday when I checked, they were scattered everywhere."

Kristina hung her head. Ms. Tyler was right. She had been in such a hurry to talk with her friends that she had left the hats in a mess.

Ms. Tyler continued, "A Drama Club supporter loaned us this collection of very special antique hats. They're perfect for our play and it's our responsibility to make sure we return

8

them in good condition. Normally we wouldn't even use them until dress rehearsal. But I thought everybody needed more practice twirling them in the dance routine."

"Oh, Ms. Tyler, I am so sorry," exclaimed Kristina. "I love our fancy hats."

"I know you do, Kristina," said Ms. Tyler. "But the Drama Club needs somebody who takes this job seriously. Do you want me to find someone else, or do you think you can do it?"

"I can do it, I promise," said Kristina. "Please give me another chance. I know I can help make the play a success!"

"Alright then, we're counting on you, Kristina. Now scoot– the hats are waiting!"

Kristina hurried over to the backstage corner where the costumes were stored. The other actors had dropped their hats on a table. Kristina carefully picked up each one and checked it for rips or stains. Then she placed all the hats on a high shelf.

Nearby, Hudson Glenn was painting a bench. Hudson was the only student without an acting role. Instead, he spent all his time working behind the scenes, mostly alone. Kristina had heard Ms. Tyler encourage him to try a small part, but Hudson had refused.

He looked over as Kristina picked up the hat

Marlee wore in the show. It was Kristina's favorite. She loved how the hat turned Marlee's beautiful eyes even bluer.

"Pink is my mom's favorite color," Hudson said, pointing to the pale pink rosebuds on the hat's blue brim. "I think you were right yesterday when you said that hat's the prettiest."

Kristina was surprised. Hudson usually didn't say much– not even to her. And they had known each other a long time. He had been a friend of hers at her old school. His family had also moved to this side of town a few months before hers had. When they were younger, Hudson talked a lot. But here at their new school, he seemed to want to be left alone.

Kristina placed Marlee's hat on the shelf and moved closer to Hudson. "Ms. Tyler just told me I had to do a better job taking care of the hats," she confided. "I've only been here a few weeks and I seem to keep messing up. But I'm going to prove that I'm a great addition to the Drama Club."

Before Hudson could answer, Kristina noticed Kyleen waving and pointing towards the exit.

"Looks like my car pool is here," Kristina said. "See you tomorrow, Hudson." She grabbed her backpack. Then she took one last look at the hats neatly lined up on the shelf and ran for the door.

# Chapter Two

**At the dinner table,** Dad gently tugged on Kristina's black braid. She had just finished telling him about Ms. Tyler's hat lecture.

"I know you'll do a great job from now on, honey," Mr. Lee said.

"Unless she gets distracted and forgets again," said Julia, Kristina's older sister.

Dad shook his head at Julia. "Nobody in this family is perfect all the time," he said. "But Kristina always does the right thing in the end. Remember the time she baked you a second birthday cake after she forgot to lock Louie out of the kitchen and he ate the first one?"

"Yeah...sorry, Kristina," mumbled Julia. Kristina smiled at her. Then she reached out to pet Louie, the Great Dane who sat eyeing her hamburger.

At school the next day, whenever Kristina

had spare time she took out her lines and repeated them over and over. By lunchtime, she knew every word by heart. Now she just had to take good care of the hats. Between bites of her peanut butter and banana sandwich, she told the other FFGs about her vow to be more responsible with her special job.

"I've looked at the hats in antique stores when I've been shopping with my mom," said Marlee. "The ones we're using are nicer than anything else I've seen." She offered Nika some of her chips.

"I almost wish I'd given up swim team practice to be in the play," said Natalie. "I can't wait to see it on Wednesday. It's going to be just great! Singing, dancing, costumes…"

Reina and Nika nodded while Natalie continued on in her enthusiastic way. Once you got Natalie started talking about something, watch out, thought Kristina. But seeing all their eager looks, Kristina felt a little jab in her stomach. Today was Friday. The play was only a few days away. What if she forgot her lines again? Was she going to look silly in front of her new friends?

By the time school was over, Kristina's fears had faded. Walking into the theater and smelling the fresh paint only made her more excited. She knew she could prove herself. She'd do such a great job in the play that the kids in Drama Club would vote her 'most improved'. She grinned as she thought about a packed audience clapping and cheering for her. But her grin vanished as soon as she saw Marlee's worried face.

Marlee grabbed Kristina's hand. "Come over here, quick," she whispered, pulling her towards the costume corner.

"What's the matter?" asked Kristina.

"It's missing," whispered Marlee. She pointed towards her own shiny brown hair. Kristina looked at Marlee's bare head, then at the hat shelf. Marlee's hat wasn't there!

"Kristina, do you think you could have forgotten to put my hat away?" asked Marlee.

"I didn't, I swear," Kristina said. "In fact, I was extra-careful with that one. You know how much I love it."

"I believe you, Marlee, but we better figure out where that hat is, fast! It's almost time for rehearsal to start."

Marlee and Kristina searched all the shelves. They combed through the fancy dresses hanging below. They even checked the boys' costumes.

Nothing. The hat with the pink rosebuds was nowhere in sight!

"I'll check onstage," whispered Marlee, while Kristina looked behind the furniture that was stacked backstage.

"Time to gather, everyone." Kristina heard Ms. Tyler calling from up front. "Marlee, you'll need your hat. And where's Kristina and Hudson?"

"Hudson is sick today," said Kyleen.

Kristina wanted to hide. But then she remembered how her dad always said he was proud of her when she did the right thing. She walked onstage.

Marlee took her hand again and whispered, "Remember, Friends Forever."

Kristina turned to the rest of the group. "I'm very sorry, Ms. Tyler," she said. "I put all the hats away really carefully last night. Now I can't find Marlee's anywhere. I know it's my responsibility. I won't stop looking until I find it!"

"I saw what a good job you did with the hats yesterday, Kristina," said Ms. Tyler. "I'm sure this isn't your fault. Let's just focus on the play for now. We don't want to waste any more practice time."

Kristina tried to stay focused during rehearsal, but all she could think about was the missing hat. Where could it be? Did Ms. Tyler really believe it wasn't her fault? What was the rest of the Drama Club thinking? With a tumble of thoughts running through her head, Kristina forgot her lines again. She also tripped during the dance routine.

Kristina wasn't the only one having problems. Starting with the missing hat, everything seemed to go wrong. Ben and Jason were goofing off behind the set and knocked over one of the plywood walls. Jason hurt his ankle, and Ms. Tyler had to call his mother. Even graceful Kyleen tipped over a can of red paint. Cameron then stepped in the paint and left a trail of shoeprints across the stage.

Ms. Tyler's cell phone rang as practice was ending. She asked the students to gather together onstage again. "I just got a call from Jason's mom," she said. "He's going to be fine, but his ankle is badly sprained. He won't be able to dance in the play. I'll have to figure something else out for the dance routine." Ms. Tyler paused while the students all let out a groan.

Then she added, "I know we had some

problems at today's rehearsal. That happens sometimes," she said. "But I want you to remember how hard you've all worked. I believe we can pull together and give the audience a real treat on Wednesday. Now go home and relax. Remember, tomorrow is Saturday, and we have an extra practice in the afternoon."

Ms. Tyler was doing her best to keep a smile on her face. Still, Kristina could see little worry lines around her eyes. Kristina looked around at the members of the Drama Club. Everyone sat silent. She knew they were all thinking the same thing she was: the play was in real trouble!

# Chapter Three

**An hour later,** Kristina flung herself full length onto the stage floorboards. She wiped a dirty hand across her sweaty forehead.

"We've looked everywhere," she groaned. "No hat!"

"I checked with the custodian," Marlee said, sitting down cross-legged next to Kristina. "The only theater trash can he emptied last night was twenty feet away from the hat shelf. There's no way the hat could have fallen into the garbage."

"I went through all the costumes again to make sure it wasn't hidden under a dress or something," said Kyleen.

"And all the students looked inside their hats during practice, just to make sure the rosebud hat didn't get stuck inside another one," Kristina added. "Plus, I looked behind every piece of furniture again and inside every drawer. That hat isn't here!"

"It was nice of Ms. Tyler to offer to stay late so we could search some more," said Marlee.

"I know," said Kristina, "that's why I hate to

have to tell her we didn't have any luck. What if she doesn't really believe that I was careful with the hats last night? What if she thinks I just can't be responsible?" She sighed so big the air fluffed her bangs off her forehead.

"We better go tell her we couldn't find it," said Marlee. "My mom agreed to come back and pick us up after we looked for the hat, and she'll be here any minute."

Ms. Tyler put her arm around Kristina. "You girls searched really hard," she said. "Now go home and quit worrying. Somehow we'll figure this all out."

Saturday morning, the Friends Forever Girls sat in a circle on the fluffy purple rug in the bedroom Kristina shared with Julia. Early morning sunshine poured through the window, turning Kyleen's red hair the color of fire. Kristina yawned. This emergency meeting was important, but her body thought it was too early to be awake on a weekend. Especially since she had slept so badly last night. First she hadn't been able to fall asleep. Then she had strange dreams all night long. In one of them, the missing rosebud hat grew wings and flew up into the clouds.

Natalie plumped up the lavender-and-green

checked pillow behind her back. "It sounds like Ms. Tyler is being nice about all this," she said. "But I bet she's pretty worried, since the play is in just a few days. I know I would be."

Kristina plunked her chin down into her hands. "I just wish I'd done a better job of proving myself up to now," she said. "I keep messing up my lines. And I did leave the hats lying around before yesterday. I wouldn't blame the other kids for thinking I'm a big dope! And I'm a little bit afraid…" Kristina's voice drifted off. Could she admit her secret fear to her new friends?

"You can tell us, Kristina," said Reina with an encouraging look.

"What if some of the kids think I stole the hat?" said Kristina. "I kept telling everyone it was my favorite. Everybody in Drama Club has been really nice to me up to now, but I'm still the new kid. For all they know, I could be a hat thief!"

"Don't think that way," said Marlee. "We know you would never do something like that and we'll help you prove it. We need to come up with a plan. I bet we can figure out where that hat is before this afternoon's play practice."

"I think some of the sports teams are

practicing at school this morning," said Natalie. "Maybe we can get somebody to drive us down so we can search for the hat again."

"It's no use," said Kristina, shaking her head. "We looked everywhere. It just isn't there."

"Maybe somebody got into the theater after play practice and took it," said Nika.

Kristina felt her stomach drop. "Oh no," she said softly.

"No, Ms. Tyler always locks the door after we leave," said Kyleen. "I've watched her. I don't think anybody could have gotten in."

"Then could somebody else who was working on the play have taken it?" asked Nika. "You know, stuffed it in their backpack and walked out with it?"

Kristina gulped. "But everybody wants the show to be a hit. Why would somebody steal the..." Kristina stopped mid-sentence. The other girls all looked at her.

"You've thought of someone, haven't you?" asked Nika.

Kristina almost said the name out loud. But then she looked at the colorful poster Marlee had made for her. It hung in a place of honor over Kristina's desk, where she could look at it from her bed. Under the painting of a beautiful butterfly was the list of Butterfly Promises– the promises the FFGs made to themselves and to their friendship. Although Kristina hadn't been a Friends Forever Girl for long, the Promises mattered to her as much as they did to the others.

Kristina knew someone who might have taken the hat. She wanted to tell the other girls so they could help her figure out how to get the hat back. But Butterfly Promise #2 said "Use kindness and be fair." What if Kristina was wrong? It wasn't fair to accuse someone of stealing without any proof.

"I'm really sorry," Kristina said to her friends. "I think I might know where to look for the hat, but I can't tell you about it without hurting somebody else. I guess this is something I have to do by myself."

The other girls got to their feet slowly.

"Are you sure you want to do this all alone?" asked Reina quietly.

Kristina nodded. Her throat was dry and her heart seemed to be beating twice as fast as normal. This is going to be one of the hardest things I've ever done, she thought.

# Chapter Four

**After her friends** had left, Kristina took Louie out into the backyard. Louie galloped around and then started sniffing near the small swing set where Kristina's two little sisters played. Kristina walked over and sat on one of the swings. She pushed back with her feet, then watched her tennis shoes scuff along the ground as she swung forward.

What were the other FFGs thinking right now? Were they upset with her? Best friends were supposed to share everything! But how could she share this?

Suddenly Kristina felt a soft motion across her cheek, something between a tickle and a kiss.

"Bella! I should have known you wouldn't leave me alone to make this decision." The beautiful butterfly fluttered around the top of Kristina's head and gently brushed against her hair.

"Right where a hat would go," said Kristina. "Are you telling me to go talk to this person about the hat? But I don't know what to say. What if I'm wrong and I hurt their feelings?"

Bella tapped against Kristina's nose: one, two, three, four, five, six, seven times.

"Butterfly Promise #7 says 'Find the courage to do what's right,'" said Kristina. "And I guess I know what that is."

Kristina waved goodbye to Bella and went back inside. She found the school directory and looked up Hudson Glenn's address. She walked into her family's home office. Her mother sat in front of the computer. Kristina looked over her mother's shoulder at a photo of a beautiful bride on the screen. "I like that one," she said. "Is that for your new customer?"

"It is. I'm glad you like it, honey," said Mom. "I'll be done working soon. What are you up to?"

"I have to do something to get ready for play practice," said Kristina. "Can I ride my bike over to Hudson Glenn's house, Mom?"

"Hudson Glenn? It's been a long time since I've seen him. His mother and I used to be friendly. I wonder how she's doing?" Mom said, leaning back in her computer chair.

"Mom, can I go?" asked Kristina again.

"Sure, sweetie, that's fine. Just be home in

time for lunch. And tell Mrs. Glenn I'll call her."

The closer she got to the Glenns' house, the slower Kristina rode. She couldn't quite believe that Hudson had taken the hat...but he was the only other person near the costume corner when she put the hat away. He had told her how pretty he thought it was. Then the hat had vanished.

Kristina thought harder. She would just ask Hudson if he had seen anything unusual after she left the theater yesterday. After all, he might have noticed something that would explain where the hat had gone. The more she considered it, the more excited she became. She was sure that Hudson would help her solve the mystery!

Kristina knocked on the Glenns' front door. She waited, but nobody answered. Just as she was turning away, she heard the door open.

"Kristina! We haven't seen you in a long time," said Mrs. Glenn.

Kristina turned back around to say hello. Instead, all she could do was stare in surprise. It sounded like Mrs. Glenn's voice. But the woman standing in the doorway didn't look at all like the Mrs. Glenn that Kristina remembered. There were dark shadows under her tired-looking eyes.

She was much thinner. And she must have cut off her long blond hair.

But that wasn't the only shock. Mrs. Glenn was wearing a fancy blue hat with pink rosebuds on the brim!

Kristina couldn't even think. What should she do next?

She heard a voice behind Mrs. Glenn. "Sorry I couldn't get the door, Mom, I was–" Hudson came rushing up. He stopped talking as soon as he saw Kristina. Then his face turned pale and he hung his head.

"Hudson, look who's here." Mrs. Glenn turned to him. "Honey, what's the matter? You look even sicker than you did yesterday. Do you have a fever?" She placed her hand across Hudson's forehead. He shook his head, but he didn't say anything.

Mrs. Glenn turned back to Kristina and gave her a long look. "Kristina, maybe you better come inside. I can tell by the look on your face that the three of us have something to talk about." She guided Kristina into the living room with one hand. Kristina noticed she had taken Hudson's hand with the other.

"Okay," said Mrs. Glenn after they were all sitting down. "It's obvious from the way you two are acting that something is going on. Who wants to tell me about it?"

Neither of them answered for a moment. Hudson finally lifted his head and looked into his mother's eyes. "Mom, I did a bad thing. When I did it, it didn't seem so wrong. But I've felt sick ever since. And I guess I probably got Kristina in trouble, too."

Mrs. Glenn put her arm around him. "Honey, what did you do? You know you'll feel better if you tell me."

Kristina stood up. "I can leave if you want me to," she said.

"No, you should stay. I owe you an apology," said Hudson. He looked down at his hands, tightly clenched in his lap. Then he looked at Kristina and started talking. His words poured out faster and faster.

"My mom is sick. She has breast cancer. Her doctor is trying to make her better, but the medicine made her hair fall out." Hudson glanced over at the pink-rosebud hat. "This hat is so pretty. I knew we didn't have enough money right now to buy anything like it. I knew it would make Mom feel better, so I took it for her. I didn't stop to think about you or the play, Kristina. I'm really sorry."

He jumped to his feet. "You deserve to be happy, Mom! You've been sick so long!"

"Oh, Hudson," said his mother. "I'm glad you realize now that what you did was wrong. You and I have an awful lot of talking to do."

Kristina stood up. "Mrs. Glenn, it's terrible that you've been so sick. I know my mom will want to help you, if she can. Is it okay if I tell her about it?"

Mrs. Glenn smiled. "Thank you, Kristina. You can tell your mother. I've missed my old friends. We don't really know the neighbors very well. I've been too tired to call people, but I didn't mean to turn this into a secret, either."

She rubbed her hand across the top of Hudson's head. "I think Hudson and I both need to reach out to other people a little more during this time," she added. "That's why I wanted him to sign up for Drama Club. I thought it would be a good way for him to make new friends."

Mrs. Glenn's smile faded. She reached up and slowly pulled off the hat. Without it, she had only a few wisps of short hair on her head. Her blue eyes looked very big in her thin face.

"Keep the hat," Kristina said. "I'll figure out some way to make it okay."

"Kristina, that's kind of you," said Mrs. Glenn. "But it doesn't belong to us. Hudson and I are going to go return it to Ms. Tyler before practice today."

"And I'll make sure everybody knows that this wasn't your fault, Kristina," said Hudson. "I'm the one they should be mad at." The Glenns followed Kristina to the door.

"Thank you for being so understanding about all this," said Mrs. Glenn. "And I hope you won't be too upset with Hudson. He needs friends right now."

"Absolutely," said Kristina. She smiled. "I think Hudson's going to find out that I'm the kind of friend who's a friend forever!"

# Chapter Five

**The Drama Club** members sat quietly as they listened to the end of Hudson's story.

"I know that my mom being sick doesn't mean it was okay for me to take the hat," he said. "And I hope you guys don't all hate me. I told Kristina I'm sorry. And now I'm telling all of you too: I'm really, really sorry."

Ms. Tyler looked at the group of students. "Does anybody want to say anything?"

Kristina jumped to her feet. "Everybody makes mistakes. I know I have. And it has been a really hard time for Hudson and his family. I think he deserves another chance."

Marlee stood up. "I'm with Kristina," she said.

"Me too!" said Kyleen. Kristina held her breath. She knew she could count on the FFGs. But what about the other Drama Club members?

One by one, the other students slowly got to their feet. Kristina breathed a big sigh of relief.

"Ms. Tyler, can I say something else?" she asked.

"Of course," said Ms. Tyler.

"I had a great idea on the way to practice," said Kristina. "If Hudson is willing to try, I think I know a way he can really help us out." Hudson looked surprised. Ms. Tyler nodded at Kristina to go on.

"What if during the performance, Jason sits over on the side of the stage and does the singing and says his lines," said Kristina, "and Hudson learns to do the dance routine in his place? I'll spend all day tomorrow practicing with him if I have to."

Hudson's eyes went big. Just as he looked like he was going to say something, Ms. Tyler spoke.

"Kristina, that's a wonderful idea. I know Jason will be so pleased to be back in the play! And it gives us a way to drag Hudson out from backstage." She smiled over at Hudson. He was shaking his head. "I'm sure you're delighted, aren't you, Hudson?"

Hudson looked at the floor. "Uh– that's a great idea, Kristina," he said in a small voice.

Ben pounded him on the back. "Thanks," he said. "And don't worry, Hudson. None of us guys are very good dancers. Mostly we just stand in one place and spin the girls around. You'll be able to learn, easy."

"Alright, then," said Ms. Tyler. "We have one more piece of business, group. We still need to focus on selling tickets. You've done a good job so far, but we still have empty seats. Remember, the Drama Club gets half of the ticket sales for a special field trip. It's your reward for working so hard. The more tickets we sell, the better that field trip can be!"

All around Kristina, people started chattering about last year's trip. They had gone to the giant amusement park three hours away.

"Okay, now, let's focus on rehearsal," Ms. Tyler said, interrupting the excited talk. "Remember, actors, the performance is only a few days away. And we have a new dancer to train."

After the Saturday practice, Kyleen's mom drove the girls straight to Nana's Grove. Natalie, Reina and Nika were already there. The FFGs spent many of their Saturday afternoons in this special spot at the end of Butterfly Lane.

Bouncing out of the van, Kristina took a long, deep breath. The fresh, sparkling air of Nana's Grove filled her lungs and cleared her head. A flash of color caught her eye as Bella floated down to land gently on her head. Then with a light brush of wings, the beautiful butterfly flitted off again. Thanks for your help, Bella, Kristina thought. I couldn't have done it without you.

She picked a rose and walked over to where Marlee was stroking her horse, Picasso. "We've been so busy with play practice we've hardly had any time for you, have we, boy?" Marlee crooned as the horse reached for Kristina's rose. Nearby, Nika sat on a tree stump, absorbed in the book she was reading. Kyleen was talking quietly with Nana Rosa. Natalie and Reina were playing with Scout, Reina's fluffy little white dog.

As Picasso finished the rose, Nana Rosa invited them all inside for some of her special hot cocoa. The smooth, creamy chocolate was a tradition for the girls, even on the sunniest day. Kristina watched as her marshmallows melted in her cup. She took a big sip and the other girls

began laughing and pointing at her upper lip. Kristina grinned. Then she stuck out her tongue as far as she could and licked off her marshmallow mustache.

Marlee handed Kristina a napkin and proclaimed, "Three cheers for Kristina! She solved the hat mystery and the Jason problem, too!"

Nana Rosa looked questioningly at Kristina. As Nana Rosa settled at the table with a cup of tea, Kristina told her the story. The other girls chimed in with details she left out. When they were finished, Nana Rosa squeezed Kristina's shoulder. "Three cheers for you, indeed!" she said. The girls and Nana Rosa let out three rousing "Hip, hip, hoorays!"

Kristina felt like the bright sun streaming through the window was shining directly into her heart. She thought she might never stop grinning. Just think, if her family hadn't moved, she would never have become an FFG. And she would not have had the Butterfly Promises to help her make a hard decision.

"I'm proud of you for sticking up for Hudson, Kristina," Nana Rosa said. "We all know that what he did was wrong. But cancer affects a whole family, not just the person who has the disease. I'm sure he's had a very rough time lately. You've been a good friend."

Reina gave Nana Rosa a thoughtful look. "It sounds like something you know about," she said.

Nana Rosa nodded. "My sister Lena had breast cancer," she said. "I understand some of the things the Glenns have been going through."

Nika set down her cocoa. "I've read about cancer," she said. "I know that it happens when cells in your body aren't normal and start to grow or even spread around. But why do people lose their hair?"

"Cancer can be tough, so the doctors use tough medicines too," said Nana Rosa. "The medicines fight the cancer, but sometimes they also fight the person's body. Patients may feel tired all the time, or sick to their stomach. And sometimes their hair falls out."

"Gosh!" Natalie sighed. "On top of everything else they have to deal with, it just doesn't seem fair! Poor Mrs. Glenn."

"Could she get a wig?" asked Marlee. "It might make her feel more like her old self."

"That was the right answer for my sister," said Nana Rosa. "But some of the other people in her cancer support group didn't like wearing a wig. They thought the wigs were hot and itchy. And they can be expensive too."

"So for some people, a hat might be better," said Reina quietly. "That explains why Hudson did what he did."

"I feel so bad for his mom. Hudson says she can't even come to the play," said Kyleen. "She has to get something called 'chemo' early this week. She'll be too sick on Wednesday." She turned to Nana Rosa and wrinkled her forehead. "I was too shy to tell Hudson that I don't know what chemo is," she admitted.

"It's a short-cut way of saying chemotherapy," said Nana Rosa. "It's the medicines that doctors use to kill cancer cells. But like I said, the treatment can make some people feel even sicker for awhile."

"I just wish there was something we could do for Mrs. Glenn," Kyleen said.

Marlee sighed. "If only we weren't so busy getting ready for the play."

Kristina had stayed quiet for awhile. While the rest were talking, she was thinking– hard. Now she jumped up and pounded her fist on the table with such a bang that the cocoa mugs jumped. "I've got it!" she cried. "I've figured out a way we can all work together to help the

Glenns. And we won't have to wait until the play is over."

# Chapter Six

**The girls spent** the rest of Saturday afternoon at Nana Rosa's cottage making plans. On Sunday afternoon they were ready to take action. Reina and Natalie headed out into the neighborhood together to sell tickets for the play.

"I'll keep babbling at them until they buy tickets just to get me to stop talking," said Natalie with a grin.

Nika started work on a special handout to give people the night of the play. Marlee began creating colorful posters. And Kyleen worked with Hudson on the dance routine, since he was going to be her partner.

Kristina herself began making phone calls. First she talked to Ms. Tyler to get permission to try the rest of their plan. Then she called all the other members of the Drama Club. One by one, she convinced them to go along with the FFGs' idea. They all agreed to keep it a secret until the night of the performance. Everything is moving forward now, thought Kristina. The Glenns are in for a huge surprise!

Ms. Tyler started Monday's practice by getting everyone together onstage. "Kristina, why don't you tell the group your news," she said.

"Some of you may know my mom is a photographer," said Kristina. "And she's agreed to use her best video camera to tape our performances." Here she turned to look at Hudson. "That way, your mom can see the whole thing even though she can't make it to the play. She'll be able to watch you onstage."

Hudson's face turned bright red and he clamped his lips together. Kristina wondered for a moment if he was going to cry, but then he nodded.

"Thanks, Kristina," he said. "I know that will make her really happy."

Kristina turned back to the Drama Club. "Plus, my mom is going to make copies of the video for us to sell to anyone who wants one," she added. "That's why Marlee made all these great posters, to help sell the videos. The money we make will go into our field trip fund."

Kristina noticed that several students smiled

at each other when she added that last part. Marlee sent her a wink. They all knew there was another piece to it, but they didn't say anything. They didn't want to spoil the surprise for Hudson.

Monday's practice went great. Kyleen and Hudson had worked so hard that he barely missed a step in the dance. But Tuesday's dress rehearsal was a nightmare. Kristina tripped over Jason's crutches and missed her lines again. The boys kept giggling at each other's stage makeup. The girls had a hard time dancing in their fancy long dresses. Marlee even dropped her hat when she twirled it. Kristina started to worry all over again about the play, but Ms. Tyler just smiled when they gathered at the end.

"That's what dress rehearsals are for," she said. "It's the last chance for everything to go wrong before the real thing. I know things will go just fine tomorrow!" Ms. Tyler continued, "Go home and get a good night's sleep. You need to be in the theater right after lunch period tomorrow to get ready for the afternoon performance for the school. Then you'll have time to relax and eat dinner before the evening performance for your parents and neighbors. Remind your families that the curtain goes up at

6:30. And here's the best news: all the tickets have been sold. We're going to have a completely full house tomorrow night!"

The members of the Drama Club cheered. Ben let out an ear-splitting whistle.

"As we say in the theater when we want to wish somebody good luck," finished Ms. Tyler, "break a leg!"

"Let's just not say it to Jason," said Kristina. "He already tried to break his leg once." Everyone laughed. Jason waved his crutches. Kristina could feel excitement bubbling like fizzy soda in her brain. The play was just a day away!

"Hey, Kyleen," she said, turning to her friend, "do you think..." But then she stopped. Kyleen's face was whiter than milk and her eyes had grown big and round.

"Kyleen, what's the matter?" asked Kristina. "Are you alright?" Marlee heard Kristina's question and hurried over too.

"Let's just get to the car, please," Kyleen whispered. "I'll tell you when we get to your house, Kristina." The FFGs were all meeting at Kristina's house to check the details of their plan one last time. Her mother had even invited them all to stay for dinner.

The ride home had never seemed as long to

The ride home had never seemed as long to Kristina. Kyleen still looked pale and unhappy. What could be wrong? Was their best singer and dancer going to miss the play because she was sick? When they reached Kristina's house, she grabbed some snacks and hurried Marlee and Kyleen upstairs to her room. The other three FFGs had already arrived and were waiting there for them.

Kristina handed a bottle of water to Kyleen. "Drink this– maybe it will make you feel better."

Kyleen sighed and took a small drink. Then she pushed away the bottle and said softly, "When Ms. Tyler said that– about a full house– something inside me just froze. It's always hard for me to perform for an audience. I've managed to hide how nervous I've been during practices, but then it was only in front of a few students." She paused and breathed deeply. "I honestly don't know if I can get up on stage in front of an audience full of people tomorrow!"

Reina and Natalie were sitting on each side of Kyleen. The two of them leaned over and gave her a squeeze at the same time.

A wave of guilt washed over Kristina. Kyleen had spent lots of time helping her when she was struggling to learn her lines. But Kristina had never even noticed her friend's stage fright. "Oh Kyleen, you're going to do a great job!" she cried. "You're the best performer we have!"

"You're a true star," Marlee said. "And you're brave, too, for facing your fear of performing in front of an audience."

"My mom has to give speeches for her job," said Nika. "She told me once that she just imagines everybody in the audience wearing pajamas. That makes her laugh so much she relaxes."

Kyleen smiled a tiny, worried smile. "Thank you," she whispered, but her eyes still looked like she had just visited a haunted house. Just then Kristina's younger sister Jess burst into the room.

"Mom says to come for dinner right now," she said, "before Louie sneaks any more of the pizza!"

The girls scrambled to their feet and headed downstairs. Kristina stopped Kyleen at the top of the stairs and gave her friend a hug.

"I believe in you," she said, stepping back and smiling at Kyleen. But inside her brain was spinning. What could they do to help Kyleen in time for the play?

# Chapter Seven

**All morning** at school the next day, students kept stopping Kristina to wish her good luck in the play. Every time it happened she felt a warm glow in her middle. But then she remembered how Kyleen had looked in the car that morning. Her face was still pale and her shoulders were hunched over. Kristina loved being the center of attention, so she did not completely understand her friend's fear. But now that she knew how Kyleen felt, she wanted to help her. She just didn't have a clue how to do it in time for the play.

Before she went to the cafeteria for lunch, Kristina hurried down to the theater. Her mother was there setting up her video camera.

"Hi, Mom. I just stopped by to see if you need anything. Thank you for doing this for us!"

"You're welcome, honey," said Mrs. Lee. "I think I'm all set. I'm glad I can do this– it's going to mean so much to Mrs. Glenn."

"Mrs. Glenn–" said Kristina. "You've just given me a great idea, Mom. I've got to run!" Kristina turned and somehow tangled her legs in the cord of the video camera.

"Be careful," said her mother with a smile. She helped Kristina untangle herself. "Remember, 'break a leg' is just a saying!"

Kristina raced into the cafeteria and looked for Kyleen. She found her frowning into a bowl of butterscotch pudding. The other FFGs looked up as Kristina skidded to a stop by their table.

"I've got it, Kyleen!" she said, sliding in next to her. Kyleen glanced up from the uneaten pudding with a puzzled look.

"Remember how you said you wished we could do something for Mrs. Glenn?" asked Kristina. Kyleen nodded.

Kristina continued, "Well, I thought of something special that only you can do." She paused a moment and then went on. "You really are the best performer in the play, Kyleen. And you're Hudson's dance partner. When Mrs. Glenn watches the video she can't help but notice you. So while you're onstage, I want you to pretend you're performing just for her. Do your very best to put a smile on her face!"

Kyleen thought for a moment. Then suddenly

she bounced in her seat. "I think you're right, Kristina," she said. "It's a special gift that I can give to her. I'm going to focus on Mrs. Glenn and forget about all those other people!"

Marlee looked over from her end of the table. "Now that you've got that worked out, you two better hurry up and eat. We have to start putting our costumes on in ten minutes for the school performance."

Getting ready for the first performance went by in a blur. Before Kristina knew it, she was standing onstage waiting for the big curtain to go up. She heard students chattering in the auditorium as they waited for the play to start. Suddenly she felt like Bella and all Bella's cousins were flying around inside her belly. She thought, so this is what people mean when they say "butterflies in your stomach." Kristina grinned. She never thought she'd get stage fright!

The curtain started to lift. Kristina looked over and watched Kyleen take a deep breath and make the thumbs-up sign behind her back. The first performance had begun!

# Chapter Eight

**After the evening** performance, Ms. Tyler stepped up onto the stage. The clapping and whistling continued. Kristina could see her parents and sisters standing on their feet and cheering. Nana Rosa was waving at her from her seat next to the other FFGs. Natalie's whistle was the loudest in the room! Clearly the nighttime audience loved the play as much as the students had earlier in the afternoon. Ms. Tyler smiled and waved her hand at the crowd.

"Ladies and gentlemen, I'd like to make an announcement," she said. She waited while the audience settled back into their seats and the clapping died down.

"I am so proud of the Drama Club," Ms. Tyler said. "You have all seen for yourselves what a splendid job they did with the play." The director paused for another burst of clapping. Then she continued, "In your program tonight you found a special handout. It gives some facts about how we can all help in the fight against cancer. One of our Drama Club families is living with cancer right now. And I am very proud to tell you that the members of the Drama Club have unanimously voted to donate all their field trip money to that family. It will help cover their extra expenses right now."

Ms. Tyler looked up and down the line of Drama Club members and then turned back to the audience. "It takes a special group of kids to give up a fun trip to help a family going through a hard time."

The parents and neighbors in the audience jumped to their feet. They began clapping and whistling again. The sound grew so loud that Kristina's ears rang. Then she looked over at Hudson. He was staring at Ms. Tyler like he couldn't believe what he had heard. Kristina grinned. It had been hard to keep the secret, but the look on Hudson's face made it worth it.

When the crowd finally stopped cheering, the curtain dropped down for the last time. Backstage, the girls all hugged each other while the boys began whooping and slapping each other on the back. The play had been an even bigger success than they had hoped.

Kristina grabbed Kyleen and gave her

another hug. "I knew you could do it," she said. "I'm so proud of you. It took guts for you to get up there in front of everybody!"

Kyleen grinned and bowed. "Now that it's over, I can admit that I was still pretty scared. When I first opened my mouth I thought I was going to croak like a bullfrog. But you were right, Kristina, I just had to focus on doing the best job I could for Mrs. Glenn."

"You both did a fantastic job," said Marlee. "Kristina, I don't think you missed a single line."

"Kristina?" said a voice behind her. Kristina turned and grabbed Hudson's hand to shake it.

"You did a great job tonight," she said. "Especially for somebody who wasn't planning to be onstage."

Hudson smiled. "I just wanted to tell you thanks one more time," he said. "I can hardly believe that the Drama Club is going to give up their field trip to help my family. And I know it was probably all your idea. You're a really good friend, Kristina!"

"You've got lots of friends now, Hudson," said Kristina. "And we're not going to let you forget it."

"I won't," he said. "But I better get home. I want to tell Mom all about the play."

Soon after Hudson left, Ms. Tyler walked up. "The person who owns the hats was here tonight," she said. "When she heard about the Drama Club donating their field trip money, she was really impressed. She'd like to donate something to the Glenns, too." Ms. Tyler pointed to the rosebud hat, still sitting on top of Marlee's shiny brown hair. "When the Drama Club takes the money and the video to Mrs. Glenn, we can also bring her this hat - to keep, this time."

The director looked at each of them. "So girls, we need someone to take care of the hat until we bring it to Mrs. Glenn. Do any of you happen to know someone who might do a good job? It has to be somebody very responsible!"

Marlee and Kyleen laughed. "I think we know just the right person, Ms. Tyler!" said Marlee. She lifted the rosebud hat off her head and handed it to Kristina.

Kristina grinned. "You can count on me," she said. "I won't let it out of my sight until it's safely on Mrs. Glenn's head!"

Here's Nika's handout:

# Help Fight Cancer!

Here are some websites where you can learn more about cancer. You can also discover some ways to help cancer patients or contribute to the fight against cancer.

This is an easy way to learn more about breast cancer: www.kidshealth.org/kid/grownup/conditions/breast_cancer.html.

If you would like to learn more about breast cancer and some of the things people are doing to help fight it, you can visit the website for an organization called Susan G. Komen for the Cure: www.komen.org.

The American Cancer Society also has lots of very good information. This website lists many ways you can help fight cancer and provides information for families who are dealing with cancer: www.cancer.org. You can also order information written specially for kids from a toll-free phone number, 1-800-ACS-2345.

Are you learning to knit? This wonderful website has free patterns to help you knit a "ChemoCap" that you can donate to a cancer patient: www.chemocaps.com.

Thank you for your support!
The Drama Club

*Here are some questions to discuss with your friends and parents, or to just think about on your own.*

1. Kristina and her family recently moved to a new home. How do you think she felt entering a new school? What do you think is the most challenging thing about meeting new people?

2. It was Kristina's responsibility to take care of the hats. At the beginning of the story she didn't pay enough attention to this task. Have you ever been asked to take care of something that didn't belong to you? Did you take it seriously? How did it make you feel when you were responsible?

3. Hudson decided to take something that wasn't his. What was the result of him stealing? Which of the Butterfly Promises did he not follow?

4. The FFG's really supported Kristina throughout the entire story. What are some ways to be a supportive friend?

5. Kristina did not tell the others what she was thinking Hudson did until after she found out what really happened. She did not gossip or spread rumors. She was treating Hudson the way she would want to be treated. What can happen when someone gossips or spreads rumors?

6. Even though Kyleen knew her lines and dance steps, she had trouble believing in herself and was nervous to perform in front of others. Have you ever felt nervous in front of other people? What did you do to get through it?

7. The Drama Club donated the money for their field trip to help a family in need. Have you ever donated money or time to a cause that you believe in? What are some other ways to help people in need?